This edition first published in 2019 by Alligator Products Ltd.
Cupcake is an imprint of Alligator Products Ltd
2nd Floor, 314 Regents Park Road, London N3 2JX
www.alligatorbooks.co.uk

Copyright © 2019 Alligator Products Ltd

Written by Katherine Sully
Illustrated by Frank Endersby

Printed in China.1528

This book belongs to

....

Hen's Feathers

cupcake

Hetta and Hilda were sisters, but not
from the same clutch of eggs. Hetta was
older than Hilda.

Hilda had plump, shiny black feathers,
sunshine yellow legs and beak,
and a beautiful red comb.

Hetta was dull and brown. But she was very kind and took good care of Hilda.

Every morning, long after the cock had crowed, the hens all waddled out of the henhouse looking for their breakfast.

Hilda was very popular with the other hens. She was always in the middle of the crowd, clucking about this and that.

On this particular morning, there was a new
hen in the yard. She had fluffy, white feathers.
Soon, everyone crowded around to meet her.

The new hen's name was Chantelle.
Everyone cooed and clucked, "What a pretty
name!" What's more, Chantelle had won a
prize at the farm show. Everyone wanted to
be her friend.

Except Hilda. Hilda sulked.

"Chantelle's prettier than me," grumbled Hilda. "And she's more popular!"

"Don't be silly, Hilda," said Hetta. "You're just as pretty as Chantelle, but in a different way."

The next morning, Hetta couldn't find Hilda anywhere. Then she spotted the other hens all crowded around Chantelle. She went over to see if Hetta was there.

"You'll never guess what," Chantelle was saying, "…the fox is back!"

There was no sign of Hilda. Now Hetta was really worried – Hilda could be in big trouble if the fox was back!

Hetta rushed all around the farmyard looking for Hilda.

"Have you seen Hilda?" she asked the pig. But he was too busy eating to reply.

"Have you seen Hilda?" she asked the farm cat. But she was too rude to even reply.

"Have you seen Hilda?" she asked the cockerel.

"She was around earlier," he crowed, "disturbing me while I was preening my feathers!"

Hetta went back to the farmyard just in time to see Hilda. She had cockerel feathers stuck to her head and tail and was strutting around the hen coop.

The other hens were giggling behind
their wings. Even Hetta had to admit
that Hilda looked silly!

That night in the henhouse, Hilda was very cross.

"I don't know why everyone thinks Chantelle's so wonderful," she snapped.

Hetta looked at her sister. "Chantelle is a very nice hen, Hilda," said Hetta.

"Just because her feathers are perfect!" grumbled Hilda.

The following morning, the hens were
all in a flutter. During the night, the fox
had been back and eggs were missing! The
hens gathered outside the henhouse. Hetta
looked around. Hilda was missing too!

"Look, over here!" called Chantelle. She had spotted cockerel feathers near a hole in the fence. They crowded around gasping and tutting. It was clear to everyone – the fox had taken Hilda.

The hens did their best to comfort Hetta.

"She was a lovely hen," they clucked. "The best sister you could have wished for."

Hetta was heartbroken!

Just then, Hilda turned up – wearing peacock
feathers. She looked ridiculous! But this time,
no one was laughing – they were too cross!

That night in the henhouse, Hilda was very upset.

"I just wanted everyone to notice me!" she hiccupped.

"You don't need all these peacock feathers, Hilda," Hetta clucked gently.
"We all love you just as you are…"

Suddenly, they heard a scuffling
and a squawking…

Hetta and Hilda rushed out of
the henhouse to find the
fox with Chantelle...
...IN HIS MOUTH!

As quick as a flash, Hilda
plucked a long peacock feather
from her tail and tickled the fox's nose.

The fox froze. His nose twitched, his eyes squeezed shut and…
…ATCHOO!

Chantelle shot from this mouth and escaped.

The next morning, the hens
gathered to hear about the night's events.
Hetta smiled to herself as she spotted Hilda.
In the middle of the crowd was her sister with
her wing around Chantelle.

"...and that's the best use for a peacock feather I know," chuckled Hilda as she told the story to her crowd of admirers one more time.

The End